VACATION IN ANTARCTICA

VACATION IN ANTARCTICA

Laura, Tamara and Marininha Klink

photographs Marina Bandeira Klink
illustrations Estúdio Zinne
translation Thomas H. Norton

Copyright© 2010 by Laura Klink, Tamara Klink and Marina Helena Klink
Copyright© 2010 Photographs by Marina Bandeira Klink
Copyright© 2012 English translation, by Thomas H. Norton

Editors
Renata Farhat Borges
Maristela Colucci

Organization
Marina Bandeira Klink

Text editors
Selma Maria
João Vilhena

English editing
Oscar Fricke
Ligia Crispino

Editorial production
Carla Arbex
Lilian Scutti

Editing of images and graphic design
Maristela Colucci

Photography
Marina Bandeira Klink

Illustrations
Estúdio Zinne

Dados Internacionais de Catalogação na Publicação (CIP) de acordo com ISBD
Oscar Garcia CRB-8/8043

Klink, Laura
    Vacation in Antártica / Laura Klink, Tamara Klink, Marininha Klink; Ilustração: Estúdio Zinne ; Fotografia: Marina Bandeira Klink ; Tradução: Thomas H. Norton. - 1. Ed. - São Paulo : Peirópolis, 2023.
    72 p. : il. ; 25 x 23 cm.

    ISBN: 978-65-5931-234-4

    1. Literatura infantojuvenil. 2. Meio ambiente. 3. Viagem. I. Klink, Tamara. II. Klink, Marininha. III. Estúdio Zinne. IV. Klink, Marina Bandeira. V. Norton, Thomas H. VI. Título.

CDD 028.5

Índice para catálogo sistemático:
1. Literatura infantojuvenil em inglês 028.5

Also available in epub version (ISBN 978-85-7596-430-9) and KF8 (ISBN 978-85-7596-441-5)

Rua Girassol, 310f – Vila Madalena
05433-000 São Paulo/SP
Tel.: (+ 55 11) 3816.0699
vendas@editorapeiropolis.com.br
www.editorapeiropolis.com.br

The first time we traveled to Antarctica with the girls on board was in February 2006. Being skipper for my own children and the children of others was a real eye opener. Sailing through unpredictable and constantly shifting scenery provides a rich and virtually nonstop learning environment. I had guessed correctly that the trip would provide a beautiful experience for the children, who by nature are full of life and curiosity. But what I had not foreseen was that we adults would learn so much, too, even though we supposedly were in the role of teachers. For over twenty years now I have traveled on a regular basis to Antarctica, but it is on the short, intensive trips we take together as a family that I learn the most. Every time I return to that continent I am reminded of how little I really know and how much more is still out there to see. My life has been a string of long journeys. Along the way I have piled up a long list of questions, had many a glove go astray, waterlogged countless pairs of boots and seen many animals whose scientific names I can barely pronounce. But I have also met many brilliant artists, authors, head-scratching researchers and daring travelers. From all of them I have learned this: there are many angles from which to see something. Beliefs I have long held and knowledge I have long thought to be settled fact are all open to reexamination — from a new angle.

This little book, which I stubbornly refused to crack open until its authors delivered it to me in its final form, is precisely that: a new way of seeing things. I am not an easy father to impress, one reason being that I am well-traveled, another being that I have also read gazillions of books. But I have to admit: I discovered in these pages more exhilarating surprises than any other book I've ever read. I am deeply proud of its authors.

Amyr Klink

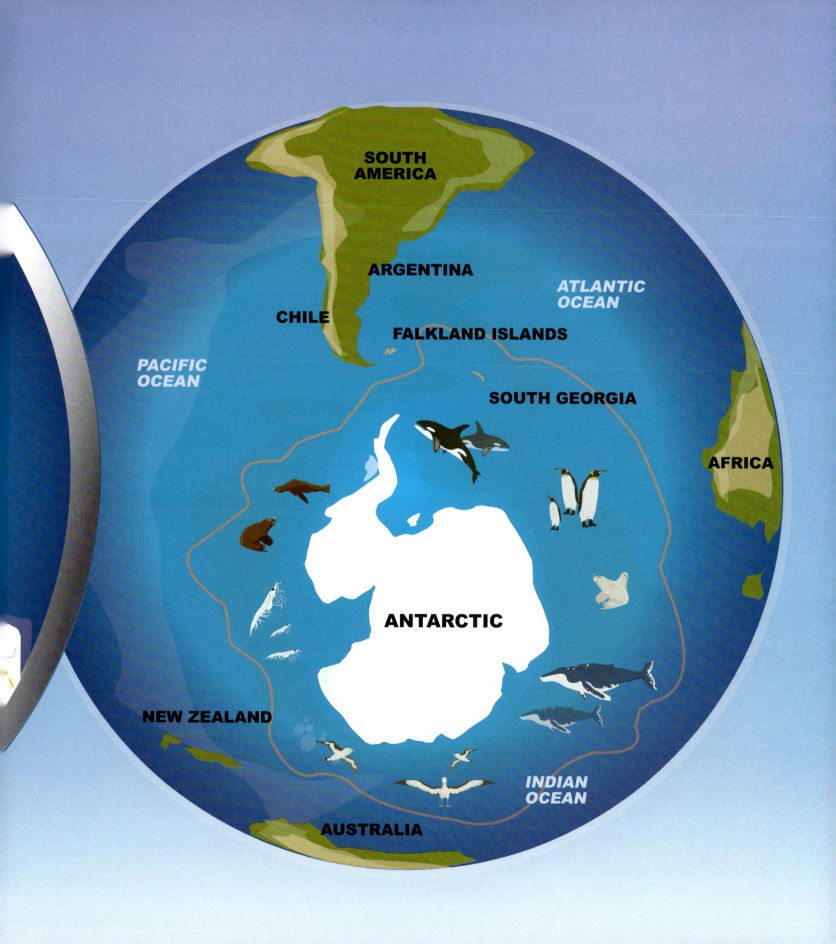

Paratii 2 is our floating home.

DEPARTURE

We were born into a family that loves to travel by boat. During our growing-up years, our father was always busy building a new sailboat. The boat's name is *Paratii 2*. It took a lot of people to build it, including some who had never even seen a boat before. Building the boat went on forever, it seemed, and the whole process took place on dry land, far from the sea. It required an enormous amount of very hard work.

When the boat was finally finished, it became instantly famous. For one thing, it quickly became known for its voyages. But it also happened to be one of the most modern sailboats in the world.

Now, our mother knew the boat was safe and that it could carry our entire family. So she asked our father if, on his next voyage, he would take us along. And he agreed! This made us happy beyond words, because every other time he had sailed away, we got left behind on the beach, just waving goodbye to our Dad.

We were happy when the long family journey finally began, but we were sad we had to leave our grandparents behind. We knew they would miss us very much. Once the boat was underway, we began to experience its unpredictable motion. It rocked and rolled and pitched and yawed, back and forth and up and down. This felt quite a bit different than what we were used to back on land. It wasn't a very pleasant sensation.

The continent of Antarctica has no owner, no flag, and no national anthem. It is a very cold place, where temperatures are practically always below freezing. We had heard that it would be boring, that all we would see was ice, ice, and more ice, and that the entire continent would be of just one color: solid white. But as we traveled we saw a very wide range of colors. And we learned that, well, there are many shades of white!

People ask us, "What do you do there?" Our answer is easy: "All sorts of things!"

Our hope is that through this book we can share with lots of other kids (and adults too!) some of the many characteristics that make Antarctica so special. We hope you have fun reading it!

SURVIVAL KIT

A good story can begin anywhere. This one began in our bedroom. Our first "exploration project" took place in our closet. We had to dig through all our stuff to find everything we would need to take with us. We're talking about lots of stuff: gloves, caps, hoods, thick clothing, and winter-layer clothes made of material that sticks to our skin. Then we had to find boots, sunglasses, sun block, and dozens of other items. We couldn't afford to forget anything because there would be no stores in Antarctica, no place to buy anything we had forgotten.

As our mother says, "There's no such thing as bad weather but… there is such a thing as the wrong clothing." She once told us a story about one of her trips. It was a very cold day in a very cold place. Mom walked past a young mother who was pushing her baby along in a stroller. As our Mom is used to seeing mothers walk their babies in strollers on a sunny, tropical day. But she couldn't believe this mother had taken her baby out for a walk on a snow-covered sidewalk in freezing temperatures! This baby should be inside a warm house! But there was really nothing for our Mom to worry about. The baby was wearing the correct clothing for that harsh winter weather.

In preparing for this voyage to Antarctica, we would have to be thinking constantly about safety. And being safe in Antarctica is a lot different from being safe in the city. In a city everything seems to be close. Sure, there are dangers, such as cars whizzing by, but the police officers are also nearby, ready to hand out tickets. But in Antarctica things would be different. On one hand, being there would set us free, yet responsibility does come with this freedom. We would be responsible for our own safety. We would have to plan well to protect ourselves from cold and hunger. To face the challenges ahead, we must always be well prepared.

CROSSING THE DRAKE PASSAGE

Crossing the Drake Passage was simply unforgettable. That's where the waters of the Pacific and Atlantic Oceans meet. The seas are really rough in that area and our stomachs felt pretty roughed-up too. When you're seasick, you don't feel like doing anything. Staying in bed all day is about all you can do. For two or three days we didn't eat anything. We drank liquids, but not too much. That was good because then we didn't need to get up so often to go to the bathroom. Crawling out of bed and staggering to the bathroom on a boat that is being tossed around by the seas – well, it's not a simple thing to do!

What about taking a shower? If you think we got to skip out on baths for all those days, well, you're exactly right! Sweat is not a problem in a cold, dry climate, so we decided to give shower a long vacation. And all the complaining that goes with baths went on vacation too!

If you were fortunate enough not to feel sick, and if you could hold steady on the swaying deck, then you were really lucky! Out on the deck, we watched in awe as birds flew in beautiful patterns over the ocean. These huge birds, petrels and albatrosses, accompanied us throughout the crossing. Petrels and albatrosses, because of their wide wingspans, enjoy flying when the winds are blowing hard. They like to soar and glide, high in the sky. They also like to skim along the surface of the water. Tiny cape doves also followed us the entire time, even when the wind wasn't blowing.

Bath day begins with my mother standing over the stove, heating water in a pot. We had to be careful not to waste the boat's freshwater reserves, so at bath time, we resorted to sponges. Freshwater must be saved because it is used for so many things, like cooking and brushing our teeth.

Tamara

Now I think I understand why my Dad once chose to spend an entire year in Antarctica – he didn't want to cross Drake Passage twice in the same year!

Marininha

HERE WE ARE!

Leaving South America behind, we sailed past the southernmost point of the continent, a famous tip of land called Cape Horn. That's how we knew we had entered Drake Passage. Though the sea ahead seemed endless, the petrels and albatrosses traveled with us all the way.

As we drew closer to Antarctica, the water temperature began to drop. In cold water, food becomes more concentrated, which causes animals to gather in greater numbers. It's as if there is a giant carousel of animals and icebergs, all floating in a giant circle around the Antarctic continent. This blue belt that encircles the continent is called the Antarctic Convergence. When we reached it, we knew we were closer to our destination and farther from home. We begin to feel that our dream voyage is actually happening!

After crossing Drake Passage – which is the worst part because everyone on the boat feels sick – we begin to feel excited in anticipation of the adventure ahead. There are signs that we are finally almost there. We no longer see albatrosses in the sky, the wind is so cold it stings the skin on our faces, and now, when we go outside, we have to wear gloves and caps. We also begin to see groups of penguins leaping out of the water and seals showing off in the sea.

When Dad said we might start seeing icebergs along the way we began spending more time outside, keeping him company in the cold. We think he enjoys feeling cold. We only like it a little bit, and quickly return to the warmth of the cabin. But seeing the first iceberg is a special event on the boat, so we have an agreement: the first person to spot an iceberg wins a prize. This encourages us to stay out in the freezing cold just a little bit longer.

As we approach Antarctica we navigate very cautiously.

When the horizon is no longer empty we can feel that we are arriving. Things begin to happen. Everything starts changing.

Tamara

One animal appears, then another, and then we see an iceberg... we're almost there!

Marininha

We can't wait to get there!

Laura

MEET THE INCREDIBLE ICEBERGS

As we get closer to Antarctica we spot more and more icebergs. Each one that appears on the horizon has a unique shape and size. They also come in different colors – and what colors! A lot of factors affect the appearance of an iceberg: the position of the sun, the conditions of the sky, the iceberg's size, the height of its face of ice, the density of the ice, and other factors. Two icebergs side-by-side can look very different from each other.

Even from a long way off it is easy to see that icebergs are not mere blocks of ice. Each is unique. It takes a while for us to get used to these color tones – white, gray, blue, and green. They are so different from the color tones we are used to seeing in Brazil. We feel as if we are watching great sculptures in the process of being made. Waves splash hard against the walls of the iceberg, carving out tips, ramps, small pools, and caves. Fingers of ice hang down in places, reminding us of stalactites. We break them off with our hands and pretend they are popsicles.

Many people know the phrase "that's just the tip of the iceberg," which means that there is a lot more to something than merely what we can see. That saying comes from the fact that only 30 percent of an iceberg's total mass is sticking out above the surface. Everybody knows this. But when you see real-life icebergs, new questions come to mind, such as: when an iceberg melts, does the lower part of it rise out of the water, or does it capsize, exposing the underside that has been under water until now?

It's hard to describe an iceberg. It has many details and it doesn't look like anything I have ever seen before. We have seen icebergs of all shapes, some look like monsters, cars, birds, dogs, and even floating castles. It's fun to watch them go by...

Marininha

Marininha and Tamara "harvest popsicles" from a wall of ice.

We didn't have paintbrushes on board, so we improvised by using our own hair!

FUN ONBOARD

The weather can change quickly in Antarctica. One minute the sun is shining and the seas are calm and smooth. Then, what seemed like paradise just a moment ago can be replaced by a fierce storm.

When the storms roll in and the wind is blowing hard we sometimes have to stay inside the cabin for hours, or even days. So we have to find something to do to keep ourselves entertained down below. We prepare skits, we play store, we invent new games, we cook, and we watch lots of movies. There's no television down there, so it's not unusual for us to watch the same movie over and over again, if we really like it. We watch some movies so many times we know them by heart!

One of the games we like to play is "pretend roller-skating." We step onto pieces of paper and slide this way and that with the movement of the boat. But sometimes we bump into things.

Playing Twister, which is even more fun on a pitching sailboat.

Concentration... it's backgammon.

Speaking in English, we taught our French friends how to make "brigadeiros".

When the weather improves we go outside to play and to see what's out there. Some games can only be played in Antarctica. For example, one game involves leaning backwards into the strong wind without falling down. We also like to break off pieces of ice hanging from rocks and pretend they are popsicles. Another game is to identify sculpted images on icebergs. You can play that same game with clouds too. We also make snow slides and snowmen. We jump from high places and fall into soft snow. We snowboard, build tunnels and hideaways in the snow. One time we even built an igloo.

Exploring ice beaches in the comfort of our dive suits.

We worked together to build an igloo.

21

We crossed the Antarctic Circle and celebrated our landing in Marguerite Bay.

On our last trip we built an igloo, with doorways and windows and all. We were all able to fit inside. We had some help from a French family that had four children that were roughly our ages. Their names were Josephine, Eliette, France and Jean-Yves. They loved coming onto our boat because we kept lots of chocolate in the cupboard! We taught them a lot of cool things about Brazil, including how to make brigadeiros (a Brazilian chocolate candy), which they had never heard of.

Laura

ONBOARD CUISINE

Sometimes serious activities can be turned into fun and games. Meal preparation on a boat can be challenging and fun at the same time. All food brought on board must be easy to prepare and to preserve. All of the ingredients must last a long time. We have to be careful with quantities because we never want to run out of food, but we don't want to waste any either.

We eat all kinds of food, including Lebanese and Japanese. Of course, what we eat the most is Brazilian food. We always carry the ingredients needed to bake cakes and bread, such as flour, yeast, salt, sugar, butter, oil, and eggs. You never want to run out of those basic ingredients!

If we ever got tired of eating orange cake, for example, we would simply make a new flavor of icing, or use a new kind of filling, just to change things up a bit. We love to eat chocolate bars and anything that contains chocolate. One person came on the boat, and seeing the contents of our cupboard, said, "This is funny, all of your food is imported, from Brazil!"

Our adventures can take place both on deck and below. We like to invent new foods and leave the kitchen all messy, with dirty pots, forks, and plates spread out everywhere. Later, we wash the dishes and swab the floor. These chores are part of the routine, as are little "accidents," such as cakes that turn out a little bit burned, pudding that never sets correctly, or minor explosions in the oven!

After having devoured all the books I brought with me, I found another book on the boat filled with recipes and advice about proper table manners. I read the entire book and decided I would try some of the recipes. But being on a boat means you have to improvise, because there's always an ingredient or two that you didn't bring along. This can be fun.

Tamara

Sometimes the wind blows really hard and the seas become very choppy. With the boat bouncing around so much, decorating a cake can be pretty tricky.

Tamara

Once we got scared. The boat got stuck on a boulder below the surface, in uncharted waters. When the boat finally came free and we began to pull away from the boulder we heard a loud BOOM! It came from the oven. We all thought we had run into another boulder. Life on a boat is full of startling incidents like that.

Tamara

Polar orange zest smoothie

Polar Orange Zest Smoothie

Ingredients:
1 can sweetened condensed milk
1 equal amount of orange juice (from concentrate is ok)
1 teaspoon orange zest
1 tray of crushed ice

Preparation:
Pour the condensed milk in a blender.
Add the orange juice.
Add the orange zest.
Blend well until creamy.
Fill six tall glasses with crushed ice.
Pour the orange cream over the ice.
Serve with a straw.

Easy to do in Antarctica, with so much handy ice!

Chocolate Cake

Ingredients:
2 eggs
1 cup of sugar
1 cup of flour
1 cup of cocoa powder
1 cup of oil
1/2 cup of hot coffee
2 teaspoons of baking powder

Preparation:
Beat the egg whites together well with a teaspoon of sugar, put aside in the refrigerator.
Whisk the egg yolks with the cup of sugar, then add the other ingredients in the order listed.
Finally, add the egg whites from the refrigerator, stirring gently.
Grease a 9" x 9" pan and add the cake batter.
Bake in oven preheated to 350 degrees F (180 degrees C) for 30 minutes.
Decorate!

TREASURE HUNT

Even as little girls we had always known that pirates spent their lives trying to find buried treasure. So we became really excited when our Dad told us, during our first trip to Antarctica, that we too would get the chance to seek buried treasure. It was a treasure Dad and some friends had buried many years earlier, in a place called Pleneau. We wondered, "Pleneau? Where is that? What could the treasure be? How will we find it under all this snow?" We were very curious, but try as we might, Dad wouldn't share any other clues.

What we did know was that when the treasure had been buried, each of our Dad's friends had chosen one thing he wanted to leave behind. We also knew that all the items had been placed in an orange box. We figured they had chosen that color so the box would be more easily found in the ice.

We had a GPS to help us, but Dad kept reminding us that we would also need some luck, because the GPS had a 10-meter margin of error. This would mean we'd have to work hard digging through all that snow! When we began to dig we had high hopes that we would quickly find what we were looking for. We dug, and dug, and dug until none of us could dig anymore. Dad kept digging alone.

The digging went on for three days. Needless to say, the only one that kept digging was our Dad. We just sat there watching, and complaining because he hadn't found anything yet. Finally, after digging an elephant-sized hole, we spotted the little orange box. We jumped and shouted.

We were met by two big surprises. One was that there was a hard sheet of ice covering the box. In other words, we could see the box, but it seemed impossible to reach. This meant even more hard work for our Dad. After great effort, we reached the box. The second surprise was that, after all that jumping and shouting, we froze, and not because it was cold. We froze because once we opened the box we saw that it contained only a whiskey bottle, a Bible, a blue rope, a tiny amount of money, and a few photos. We were disappointed. Marininha asked, "But, Dad, where are the jewels, the pearls, and the diamond necklaces?"

This feeling of disappointment lasted for several days because finding the box had required so much hard work. But then we had an idea: why not leave another treasure buried in the same place? So we gathered a few of our own favorite items – toys, hair clips, and drawings we had made. This would give us a good reason to come back here. This treasure was ours, and Dad helped us bury it in a secret place. This would indeed be a true treasure for us to find when we returned to this place.

It took us three days of digging to finally uncover the hidden treasure.

SEALS

There are several species of seals in the world. Six species live in the region below the Antarctic Convergence. There are no animals that live in Antarctica all year long, and this is true of seals too. They travel there during the summer months, and spend their winters at sea. Seals species are distributed in a concentric ring around the Antarctic shoreline, and the only seal that spends all winter ashore in Antarctica is the Weddell Seal.

On our trip, we saw leopard seals, crabeater seals, Weddell seals, fur seals (which are also called sea lions), and elephant seals. The only species we did not see up close was the Ross seal.

After many trips, we now have good seal-recognition skills. The leopard seal has a face that resembles a giant snake. It is the only seal that eats penguins, and it does so in a unique way. With strong neck muscles and huge jaws, the leopard seal opens its wide mouth and sinks its sharp teeth into its prey. Next, it shakes the penguin violently from side to side, ripping its skin off at the same time so it can eat the meat.

Weddell seals have a spotted coat. This is the only seal species that spends the entire winter in Antarctica. In order to reach their main source of food, known as krill, they must break through the ice that forms on the surface of the sea.

Crabeater seals may have gotten their name because the first humans to see them mistakenly thought they eat crabs. The truth is that krill is their main diet, too.

Antarctic sea lions, also known as fur seals, are the only species whose ears are visible. Their whiskers are very important because they serve as antenna to help the sea lions find food. When fish swim they cause underwater vibration. The fur seal's whiskers sense those vibrations, and then the fur seal follows the vibrations to their source – which often becomes its next meal.

It's fun to hang out with fur seals, but we have to be careful not to get bitten. They don't brush their teeth, so their mouths are full of nasty bacteria. A bite, in addition to being very painful, could lead to a bad infection. Some people have died from fur seal bites.

Elephant seals are huge! They spend eight months at sea, diving over 2,000 feet deep in search of food. They have very large eyes that allow them to see in places too deep for the sunlight to reach. Their dark skin absorbs heat during the summer as they rest on the beach, shedding their skin and hair. They toss sand onto their backs to protect their skin from damaging sun rays.

> One day, two fur seals charged toward us. At first we thought they wanted to play, but then we found out they were actually defending their territory. They thought we were invaders. To fend them off we had to slap our hands and feet on the water, which startled them. They turned around and left us alone.
>
> Laura

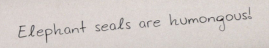

Elephant seals are humongous!

Laura and a lazy Weddell seal.

We had to keep an eye on the fur seals because they are fast, and could bite us.

Crabeater seals are very docile.

Even when it is resting, the gaze of a leopard seal can be a bit frightening.

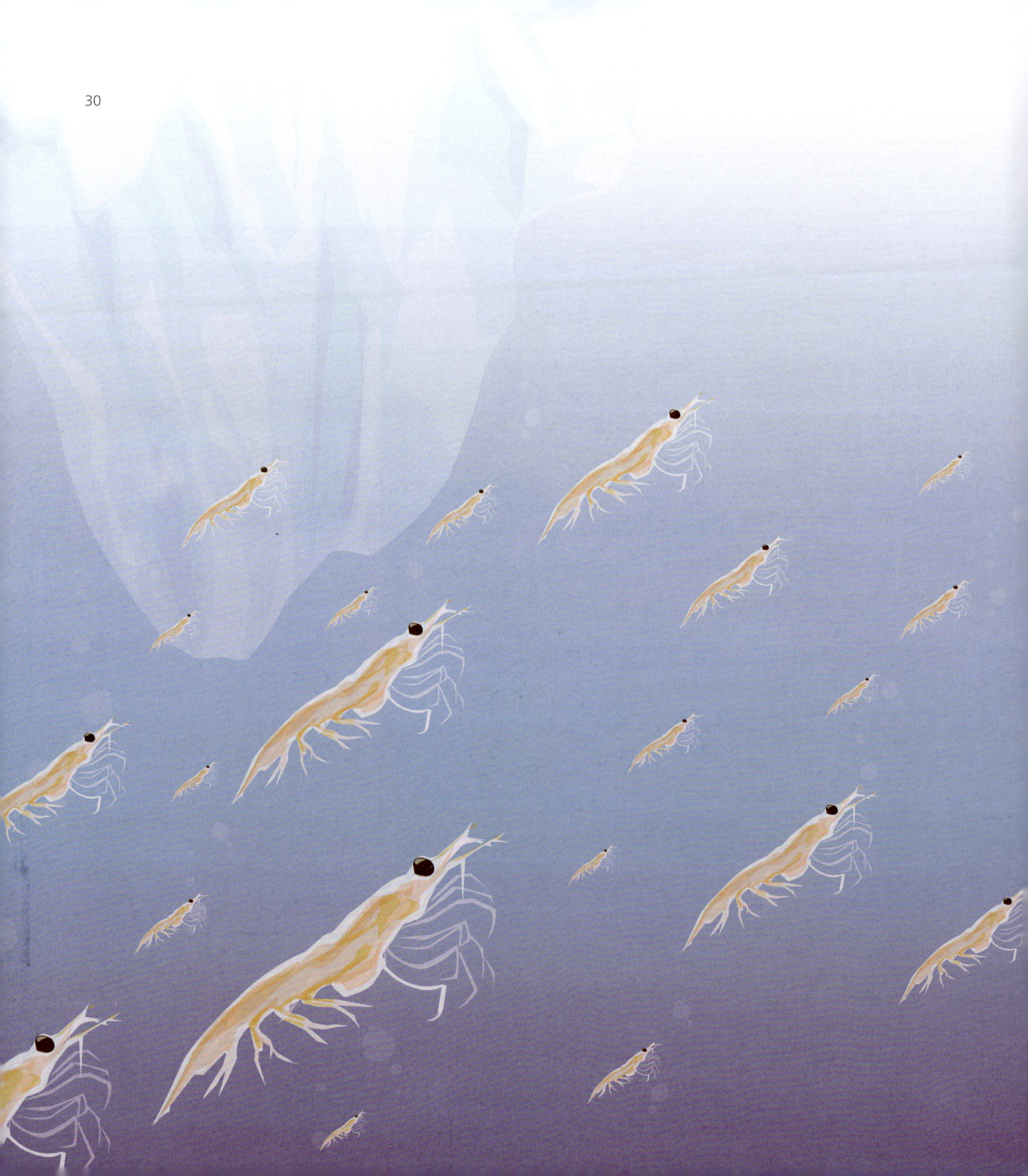

SIZE DOESN'T MATTER

Krill are tiny shrimp, less than two inches long. They're tiny, but also very important because krill is the foundation to the food chain in Antarctica. All Antarctic animals eat krill: penguins, seals, and even whales. If all the krill were to die, every other animal that feeds off krill would die too. The problem is that there's always someone out there who thinks he or she can do whatever they want with nature. We wonder how long will humans continue in this kind of behavior? Will there always be companies that try to make money from the raw materials Earth contains?

Some countries see krill as a huge source of money. They fish the krill and use it as food for small fish farms and even aquarium fish. But just think about how many sources of food an aquarium fish has compared to the scarce food supply available in Antarctica. There could come a day when the krill have been killed off. If that happens, all the wildlife in Antarctica will die too.

WHALE SOUP

Imagine an animal whose heart is the size of a Mini Cooper car, whose tongue weighs as much as an elephant, but whose location you can never know. This animal is very calm, swims well, and suddenly appears right up next to us. And we never sense its arrival. We're talking about whales.

We humans began to create problems for whales back when we discovered that all their body parts could be useful to us in some way or another. Men began to hunt them with increasing intensity back when the world knew nothing of vegetable oil and needed animal fat. Not to mention, whales are loaded with meat, oil, bones, and fins. The whale population began to decrease quickly.

Whales take years to multiply, and for a long time they were disappearing faster than new whales were being born. Finally, we humans became concerned about this.

Whales have plenty of room to roam in Antarctica. But that has not always been the case. The whales we saw were actually the grandchildren of the survivors of that great whale-hunting age. Because humans thought they could hunt at will, many whale species almost became endangered to extinction.

In 1986, many countries (including Brazil) put into practice an agreement, which was signed in 1982, that prohibits the commercial hunting of whales. But some countries did not sign the agreement and continue to hunt whales to this day. Some of them claim they hunt whales for cultural reasons, others say they do it for scientific research. But if you ever happen to visit a restaurant in one of those countries, just take a peek at the menu and you'll see the real reason they still hunt whales.

One early morning we saw jets of spray in the air. Suddenly, a whale emerged very close to the boat, followed by a group of four, five — lots of them! They circled the boat. There were so many we couldn't count them; it looked like hundreds of them. The sea roiled like a pot full of humpback-whale soup. They swam so close to the boat that it began to pitch and roll. I will never forget that day.

Laura

We learned why people talk of "whale hunting." If they live in the sea, why don't we say "whale fishing"? Well there is a simple reason: whales are mammals, and mammals get hunted. Fish get fished.

Whales breathe the same oxygen we do, while fish breathe underwater, absorbing oxygen through their gills. Females breastfeed their young (called "calves") underwater. A whale calf can gobble up to 25 gallons of milk per day. That's amazing, isn't it?

The blue whale is the largest mammal on Earth. The longest ever measured was around 110 feet in length. We were disappointed that we didn't get to see a blue whale up close.

There are two kinds of whales, baleen whales and toothed whales.

Baleen whales feed on krill, but some also eat crustaceans and some types of shellfish. They don't eat penguins or seals, because they don't have teeth with which to chew. Instead of teeth, these whales have a row of thin plates called "baleen" on the upper side of their jaws. They're made of the same material as our fingernails. Biologists classify these whales as *Mysticeti*.

While visiting the southern Brazilian state of Santa Catarina we learned that you don't have to be at sea to spot a whale! We sat in the sand and watched them blow through their spouts while they played very near the beach. We also visited the Right Whale Project research center, where we learned why the whales sometimes come close to the shore.

Laura

Whales are migratory animals. Some come to Brazil during the winter, seeking warmer water so they can reproduce and protect their calves while they are still babies. They leave in the springtime, after the breastfeeding period. Calves continue to breastfeed on the journey back to Antarctica, but their mothers wean them after they have learned how to catch their own food.

Right whales swim to Brazil to spend their winters off the coast of the state of Santa Catarina, keeping their young near the shore to protect them from predators.

Right whales have a unique way of eating krill and small fish. They swim along the surface with their mouths wide open, scooping up food and water. Then they close their mouths and push the water out through the baleen. All that's left is food.

Whales are my favorite animals because they are so mysterious. You never know where they are or what they will do.

Tamara

Humpback whales are very active and leap high out of the water. During the winter, humpbacks migrate from the region of South Georgia Island to the southern part of the Brazilian state of Bahia, in the region of the *Abrolhos* archipelago. We learned from the staff at the Humpback Whale Institute that a single whale weighs as much as eight elephants (90,000 pounds!), and that they make really strange sounds underwater.

While we were in Antarctica we saw humpback whales feeding by using a technique called a "bubble net." They dive deep and release air bubbles into the water. Krill and tiny fish get trapped in the bubbles. Then, the whales just scoop the bubbles into their huge mouths, get rid of the water through their baleen, and swallow their meal!

When we see a humpback whale close-up, we are amazed at how large it is and that it doesn't seem to be afraid of us. Some even passed slowly back and forth under the boat.

Laura

Orca whales sit at the top of the food chain in Antarctica. They are not *Mysticeti*, which means they don't use baleen to sift out water from their food. Orcas are *Odondoceti*, which means they have actual teeth.

Orcas are voracious eaters. They eat about 250 kilograms of food per day (that's 550 pounds!) and can weigh as much as 20,000 pounds. They feed on fish, penguins, squid, seals – and even whales! They always swim in a pod of up to 50 family members. That explains why they are so skilled at killing whales. They get organized and swim in a circle around the whale until it grows tired, and then they attack. They are interested mostly in eating the whale's tongue. After they're finished with it, they leave the dead whale's body floating in the sea.

Humans tend to see orca whales as mean (humans sometimes call the orca a "killer whale"), but they aren't really mean at all. On one of our trips to Antarctica we heard of a group of orca whales swimming alongside another sailboat. One of the "killer" whales and its calf came very close to the back (or "stern") of the boat, where a young boy was sitting. He got a good look at the mother, who raised her head far out of the water and held still, looking at the boy as if to show how proud she was of her own child. They were so close he could almost touch them. Then, she and her baby swam away.

There have been cases of orcas attacking humans, but they probably did not have the intention to kill. It may have happened because they do not understand that humans cannot breathe underwater.

Sperm whales are also *Odontoceti*, toothed whales like orcas and dolphins. Sperm whales are very difficult to spot because they like to go deep. They can dive over 9,000 feet deep and hold their breath for over an hour. They feed on giant squid, which is quite an easy prey for them. Sperm whales like to swim alone and, when they find a giant squid, they bite it, which causes the squid instinctively to suction itself over the whale's face, in an attempt to escape. But the whale simply rises quickly toward the surface of the water. The changes in pressure are so rapid and violent that the squid dies on the way up. Then, the sperm whale can take all the time in the world to eat its meal.

It's exciting to see a humpback whale make a dive!

Humpbacks follow us in Antarctica

A skeleton of a sperm whale was assembled by the film team of the famous oceanographer, Jacques Cousteau, who was the first man to dive below the ice in Antarctica. In 1975, Cousteau visited Antarctica and produced documentaries that included scenes taken on land, underwater, and from the sky.

Laura

By "getting inside the head" of a whale we get a feeling of how big they are, compared to us.

Laura and Tamara take a look at a reconstructed skeleton on King George Island.

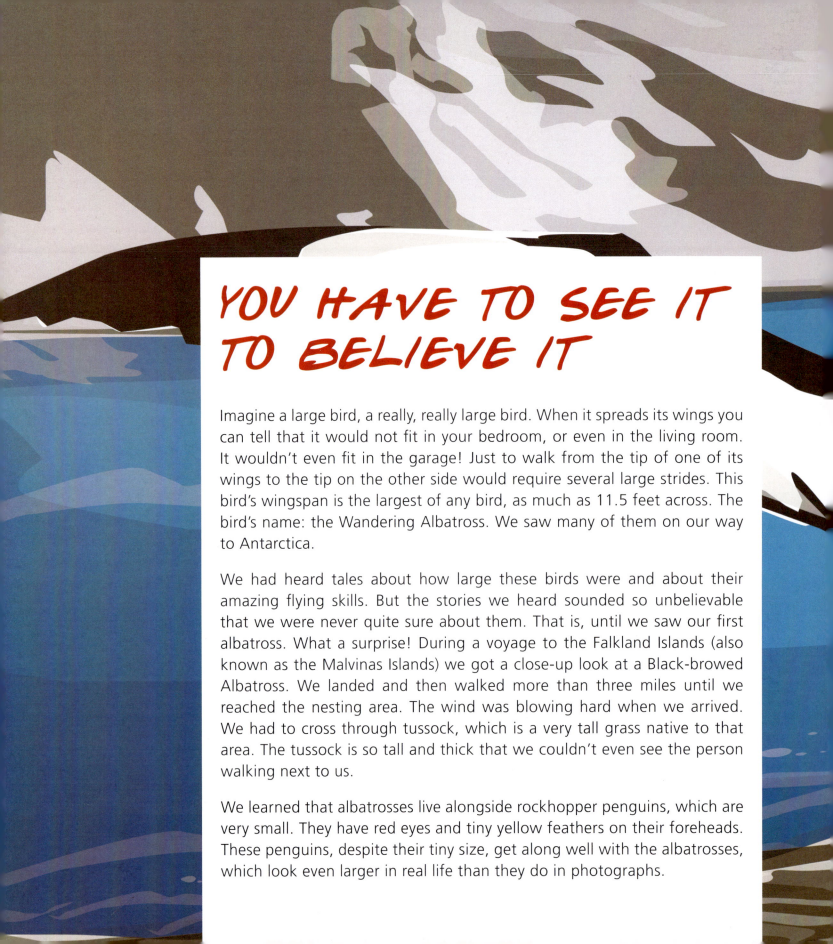

YOU HAVE TO SEE IT TO BELIEVE IT

Imagine a large bird, a really, really large bird. When it spreads its wings you can tell that it would not fit in your bedroom, or even in the living room. It wouldn't even fit in the garage! Just to walk from the tip of one of its wings to the tip on the other side would require several large strides. This bird's wingspan is the largest of any bird, as much as 11.5 feet across. The bird's name: the Wandering Albatross. We saw many of them on our way to Antarctica.

We had heard tales about how large these birds were and about their amazing flying skills. But the stories we heard sounded so unbelievable that we were never quite sure about them. That is, until we saw our first albatross. What a surprise! During a voyage to the Falkland Islands (also known as the Malvinas Islands) we got a close-up look at a Black-browed Albatross. We landed and then walked more than three miles until we reached the nesting area. The wind was blowing hard when we arrived. We had to cross through tussock, which is a very tall grass native to that area. The tussock is so tall and thick that we couldn't even see the person walking next to us.

We learned that albatrosses live alongside rockhopper penguins, which are very small. They have red eyes and tiny yellow feathers on their foreheads. These penguins, despite their tiny size, get along well with the albatrosses, which look even larger in real life than they do in photographs.

All it takes is one look at the Black-browed Albatross to understand how it got its name.

The Wandering Albatross likes to glide for long distances across the ocean, carried by the strong win[d]

Albatrosses spend most of the year in flight, but they always return to the same island for reproduction. The way they fly is a lesson in how these birds have adapted to their environment. They are so large that if they had to flap their wings all the time they would waste too much energy, so they flap their wings just a few times until the strong wind lifts them, and then they begin to glide and soar, without flapping their wings at all. This is quite different from, say, a hummingbird, which flaps its wings constantly in order to stay in the air. Any time you see an albatross on land, you can be sure strong winds blow near where he's standing.

From the sky albatrosses can see everything down below, such as the tiny fish and krill on which they feed. These are fishing birds, so they get their food out on the high seas. Albatrosses have nasal tubes that run along the tops of their beaks. When they fish, they inevitably scoop up water too. Like the whales, they get rid of the water and keep the food. But albatrosses blow the water out through their nasal tubes.

PARENTS AND CHILDREN ARE ALL ALIKE

We discovered a lot of things on our voyages, among which is this: there is a lot we can learn from animals.

We learned a lesson from albatrosses. Under normal conditions they live to be about 70 years old, about the same as humans. They reproduce every two years. It takes eight or nine months for their young to learn to fly, and only then do they head out to find their own food. Albatrosses build their nests high atop cliffs, which seemed a bit illogical until we learned the reason why.

Think about it: we begin as babies, and then we become toddlers. How many years have to go by before we can do things without the help of our parents? But a day finally arrives when we must grow up and learn to do the things adults do. Baby albatrosses also have to grow up, but if they're the least bit scared, their parents give them a little "push."

The downy fluff that covers a baby albatross takes months to fall away. This downy fluff is not waterproof, so if the baby bird falls into the water it will drown. With time, the down fluff falls away and feathers grow in. Throughout this period, the baby albatross will practice its flight skills, opening and flapping its wings, and jumping up and down in the nest. This goes on until its parents determine that their baby is ready to make its first flight.

> With albatrosses and with all animals that live in Antarctica, we've learned that by taking a voyage you can learn a lot that you would never learn at school.
>
> Laura, Tamara and Marininha

Like us, when as babies we are afraid to take our first steps, albatrosses are afraid to take their first flight. But the parent birds cannot wait too long because seeking food for a growing baby albatross is no easy task. Some birds tear up their nest when they see that their young are getting big. This way the young birds have to fly off and seek their own food. In the case of albatrosses, if the baby birds don't fly away on their own, the parents push them from the cliff-tops! That's why they build their nests so high, so the young birds will figure out how to fly while they are in free-fall. As they fall they notice that all they have to do is open those enormous wings and catch the wind just right. If they don't figure it out quickly, they die. But they would die of hunger if they stayed in their nests and never attempted to fly. Once in flight, they become true albatrosses, prepared to join their parents and do the things adults do.

Albatrosses cover incredible distances. They are born on sub-Antarctic islands and sometimes end up flying a full circle around the entire continent. They fly over the sea that separates South America from Antarctica, and sometimes as far north as Brazil, just seeking food. Unfortunately, this carries some risk: to the albatross, anything that floats is food, which means they sometimes end up eating plastic bottle caps, nylon string, plastic bags, and other trash people toss into the sea, items that spend years floating around on the currents. That's not to mention the times they end up swallowing big spools of fishing line or fishhooks. Many albatrosses die every day like this and never make it back to their nests where their babies are left to die alone.

> Trash belongs in a trash can and not on the ground or sidewalk. Before tossing trash onto the ground everyone should think about a simple plastic bottle cap, which seems so inoffensive but that can end up in the stomach of an albatross and end its life.
>
> Laura

It's a beautiful thing to see an albatross fly overhead.

Laura

A baby albatross trying out its wings while still in the nest.

It's not unusual to see a penguin raising two babies at a time.

King penguins live in sub-Antarctic regions and are quite noisy. They shout over each other to get everyone's attention.

THE WORLD OF PENGUINS

When we speak about the animals of Antarctica or from cold regions, many people remember polar bears and penguins. But we have to say something very important: polar bears live on the other side of the world, near the North Pole, where penguins are not to be found at all. There are many types of penguins that live spread out all over the southern part of the globe: the Antarctic region, the Falkland Islands, South America and even in South Africa.

Penguins do not like to hang out alone. They know that if they stay in groups their chances of survival improve. So they live in huge colonies made up of hundreds or even thousands of penguins. These places are called rookeries and reflect the way penguins have adapted to their environment. Rookeries are normally located very near the ocean, so the penguins can have easy access to food.

Penguins are Antarctica's most popular animal. Their fame reaches so far around the world that we even have a friend that keeps a little penguin doll on top of her refrigerator. We watch penguins in movies and cartoons, and at school our teachers talk about them any time they mention the frozen regions of the world. Sometimes we see the image of a penguin on a logo of frozen foods at the supermarket. But there's a lot more to know about penguins.

For starters, penguins are birds. Some of you might say, "But they don't fly!" Well, by the way scientists define it, birds are feathered animals. And penguins have feathers. It's true they don't fly because their wings are adapted for swimming. They are the only birds that swim instead of flying, which is why so many people get confused and think they are not birds.

The surface of a penguin's body is very smooth, covered by a coat of tightly-packed little feathers that are designed to keep water from touching the penguin's skin, which is also protected by a thick layer of fat. Baby penguins, or "chicks," are about the size of a baby chicken and are born covered in a downy fluff that protects them from the cold. It is easy to tell the different species apart by looking at the chicks, because while they are young they look very different from their cousins.

Penguins eat fish, squid, krill and small shellfish. If you look closely at a penguin in its nest you will see that its tongue looks like a toothbrush. Food sticks to its tongue and makes it easy to swallow.

We learned that when a penguin eats, it sorts out the food into two portions. The first portion is for the chicks and the second portion heads on down into the penguin's stomach. But if the parents run sort of food for their chicks, they can regurgitate their own food.

Penguins have a variety of colors on their bodies: black and white! The purpose of their coloring scheme is camouflage, to protect them from predators. They are difficult to see in the water because of their black backsides. When they stand on land they show their white chests, blending in with the snow.

Tamara in a Gentoo penguin rookery.

An Adélie penguin

Gentoo penguins

A Chinstrap penguin

The Magellanic penguin lives on the Falkland Islands and in other locations in South America.

The Rockhopper penguin lives on the Falkland Islands.

Magellanic penguins are black with white bands on their bodies. They live on dry land in very large groups and build their nests in holes in the ground. Some groups that live in South America get carried by the currents all the way to the beaches of Brazil. When this happens, people often feel the urge to carry them to some cold place so they can feel something like normal temperatures. But that's not a good idea. Penguins burn a lot of energy and fat making that long journey. In fact, they are probably feeling very cold, weak, and undernourished. So what they need is to be wrapped in blankets and kept warm. The next step is to find an animal conservation organization as quickly as possible. They will know how to take the penguins back home.

Sometimes ships, airplanes, or helicopters are used to carrying them back to their homes, to zoos, or to aquariums, where they can be rehabilitated and set free to return home on their own. But every now and then a penguin will have to stay under the care of the zoo or aquarium for so long that they end up just staying there. But that gives us a chance to learn about them.

A Gentoo penguin caring for its young in a rocky nest on the Antarctica Peninsula.

In Antarctica, penguin nests are built out of pebbles. An adult penguin will walk long distances to pick up a single pebble, which it brings back to the nest with its beak. There are thieves among penguins. Sometimes, when the adults are off looking for pebbles, neighbor penguins sneak over and steal the ones already in place. When the owner of the nest returns they get into a big fight. The pebbles are very important to penguins. If they don't find enough of them, their nest won't be large enough to incubate their eggs. That's why we knew we shouldn't pick up any little rocks or pebbles from there, even though we would have liked to bring one home.

Laura

54

All we had to do was sit still and, before long, a curious penguin would waddle over to see us.

In Antarctica animals came up very close to us!

Laura

One day, as my mother was taking photographs, a penguin crawled into her backpack. Penguins are curious by nature, but I think that one was actually feeling cold!

Marininha

> The weather in Antarctica changes very quickly. One day, Tamara was playing out on the deck of the boat, wearing only a tee-shirt and normal pants. Within seconds, the weather changed and we witnessed the fiercest windstorm of the whole trip...
>
> Marininha

FRIGHTENING MOMENTS

Once we crossed the Antarctic Convergence line, we began to have mixed feelings. We were anxious to step onto firm land again, but at the same time we were worried. We had often heard the adults talk about how important it is to be well-prepared before making a trip to Antarctica. Because we were so very far from any cities, we knew we could not count on help from other people. So it worried us a little bit not to know what we would encounter ahead, aware that some things do not even show up on maps. Submerged rocks can sink a boat, or at least badly damage it. So we had to be well-prepared and trust the people traveling with us.

One day we were making preparations for Flavio's birthday party. We baked a cake and were making *brigadeiros* when, suddenly, all the silverware went flying across the boat! We heard the belly of the boat scraping against rocks. We all ran outside to see what had happened. We had run aground in only 18 inches of water! We were lucky we had a strong aluminum boat. It took a great deal of work and effort to get the boat free again. Our Dad steered "our house" and Flavio worked from the small inflatable boat, wiggling the boat this way and that to get us off the rocks (which didn't appear on any nautical charts). The waves pushed the boat back and forth. Finally, the boat tilted sideways, and remained there, leaning over on its side. Then it crashed down into the water with a huge boom! The force of the boat on the water created another round of waves. It took a long while, but we finally got out of there.

In another occasion, we were leaving Dorian Bay in the morning, headed for the Lemair Channel. No one knows exactly what happened, but our Dad suddenly started yelling. We followed him up on deck. It turns out that he had thought Flavio was at the helm (steering the boat), so our Dad went to check on the meteorology (now there's a long word!) below deck. Everything happened very quickly. When Dad looked out the window he saw that we were headed straight for a collision with an iceberg! So he ran up, shouting. Fortunately, he was able to turn the rudder and prevent a disaster that could have sunk *Paratii 2*. And, from where we were at that moment, hitching a ride home would not have been very easy!

We got face-to-face with leopard seals; walked by multitudes of penguins; slid down natural ice slides; and sailed alone in a little Optimist sailboat. Courage was required to do all of this. People often talk about courage as if it is something you build or create. Our trips have taught me that courage is inside us. What we must learn to do is to bring it out from inside.

Tamara

There was one really bad night. Mom told us the heavy anchor chain was scraping across the rocks at the bottom of the bay, hauled back and forth by the currents. This caused the lines on the boat to stretch tight and the boat seemed to dance this way and that. During the night a huge iceberg broke into pieces, all of which found their way to the channel entrance, closing off the route we had used to come into the bay.

Tamara

THE LITTLE OPTIMIST

An Optimist is a tiny sailboat, the smallest sailboat of all. We learned to sail in our first Optimist when we were seven and ten years old (remember, two of us – Tamara and Laura – are twins). When we traveled to Antarctica in 2010, Mom surprised us. She had hidden an Optimist inside *Paratii 2* and didn't reveal her secret until we were sailing peacefully across Margarita Bay, at the southernmost end of the Antarctic Peninsula, surrounded by icebergs. It was a sunny morning and the wind was very light. She assembled the boat and put it into the water. We left *Paratii 2* in the tiny Optimist and sailed in between and around those giant icebergs!

> In the huge expanse of blue the little yellow boat seemed so tiny! No wind was blowing so I leaned against the sides of the boat and just looked out at the blue and white scenery all around me. Penguins, which swim at incredible speeds and only come out of the water to breathe, were all around me. Two of them followed me, as if curious to see what that strange creature, moving as slow as the wind, was up to.
>
> Tamara

Tamara sailing around the icebergs.

Marininha was the first to sail the Optimist, but she didn't sail for very long. Next, it was my turn. I passed alongside a mini-iceberg with three Crabeater seals. Next, I passed by an iceberg that had Adelie penguins. I kept going and passed several huge icebergs. It was unbelievable! I sailed for a good while before turning back for the inflatable boat, where my parents and sisters were waiting for me. When I was getting close to them, I heard Marininha shout: "Laura, a leopard seal, a leopard seal!"

Lucky Laura got a good close-up look at some Adélie penguins.

Marininha, who was just 10 years old, was the first to sail the Optimist in Antarctica.

It was right next to me, and I got scared. I tied the towline quickly and the inflatable started towing me away. Suddenly, I looked down and saw that the leopard seal was right next to me again. I screamed. It scared me to death! I really didn't think the leopard seal would follow alongside me. But I think my scream scared her because she went under the water and disappeared. When I calmed down, there she was again, following me! I have never seen a head like that. It was enormous! Three times the size of a person's head!

Laura

NO DISAPPOINTMENT HERE

Near Antarctica there is a place everyone should get to know: Deception Island. In Portuguese (the language we speak in Brazil), the word "decepção" means "disappointment." But there was nothing disappointing about that place. It is an island formed by a volcano. What's amazing about the island is that we were able to sail right into the middle of it through a gap in the volcano's wall that formed a long, long time ago. We sailed right into the center of the submerged volcanic crater! On a windless day the waters are very calm. We were able to get off the boat inside the crater.

It's no big deal to see a photo of someone running barefoot along the beach in a bikini. But despite the freezing water, blocks of ice, and snow-covered mountains, we had to run on this beach just to keep from burning our feet! The rocks and thick, black sand that cover the beach are very hot, hot enough to heat the water in shallow areas making it warm enough to go swimming!

> I jump up and down to keep from burning the soles of my feet on the ground, but when I step into the frigid water I get nervous, wondering whether I should start floating or keep walking in a bit deeper. I try to stand still in the warm spots, but the currents are strong and it's hard to stay in one place!
>
> Laura

The air was freezing, the water was steaming hot, and my feet burned from the hot volcanic sand!

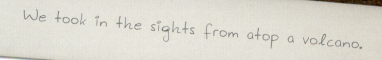

We took in the sights from atop a volcano.

BACK HOME

Back in our bedroom, having returned from our first trip to Antarctica, we came to realize that our beloved mix of stuffed animals would never actually be able to get along or live together. By traveling to Antarctica, in addition to learning that dogs are not allowed, we came to realize that polar bears only live close to the North Pole and penguins only live close to the South Pole. We learned the whales and sharks, despite the fact that both live in the sea, never meet. And lions and hippopotamuses live in African forests, not in Brazil.

The word "ecosystem" refers to systems of nature across the planet in which every living thing has a place and a function determined by the particular climate, vegetation and available food sources of that place. Of course, animals got adapted to it a long time ago and would be living together freely if humans had not come along and gone overboard with their own desires and needs…

As we draw close to Brazil again, we can still see some of the sea birds we saw below the Antarctic Convergence – albatrosses!

We see many plastic objects, large and small, floating on the water. We know that to a sea bird anything that floats is food, so they end up eating thousands of little bits of plastic and other trash they find floating along the surface.

We also see hundreds of plastic bags, which pose a huge danger to sea turtles, who confuse them for jellyfish and swallow them whole and then die of starvation.

Animals are victims of our attitudes, and that includes animals that live in the sea. Each time we toss a bottle cap or plastic bag onto the sidewalk, we should remember that litter travels down paths we might never imagine. Something I toss on the sidewalk in the big city today could end up floating on the sea tomorrow. If we are not careful we could be causing the deaths of thousands of animals that live far away from us.

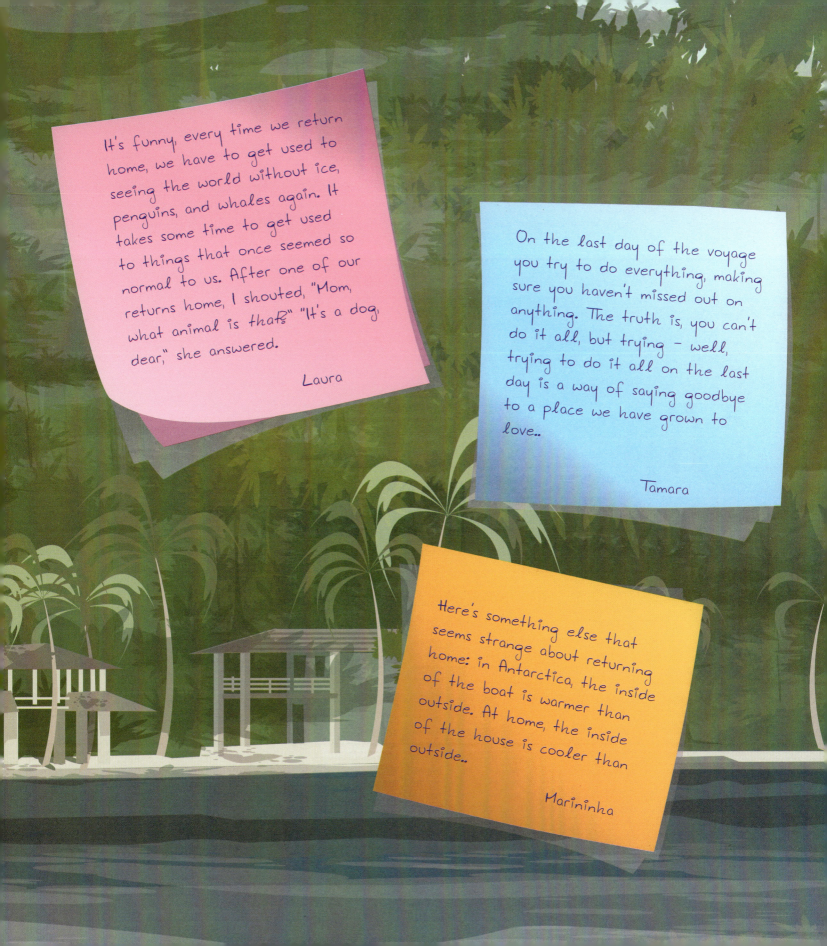

It's funny, every time we return home, we have to get used to seeing the world without ice, penguins, and whales again. It takes some time to get used to things that once seemed so normal to us. After one of our returns home, I shouted, "Mom, what animal is that?" "It's a dog, dear," she answered.

Laura

On the last day of the voyage you try to do everything, making sure you haven't missed out on anything. The truth is, you can't do it all, but trying — well, trying to do it all on the last day is a way of saying goodbye to a place we have grown to love..

Tamara

Here's something else that seems strange about returning home: in Antarctica, the inside of the boat is warmer than outside. At home, the inside of the house is cooler than outside..

Marininha

THE AUTORS BY THEMSELVES

Laura Klink, 13 years old.

Tamara Klink, 13 years old and Laura's twin.

Marininha Klink, 10 years old – the youngest of the three.

Laura enjoys photography and can spot details everyone else seems to miss.

Tamara loves to cook and try her hand at new recipes.

Marininha likes to wash the dishes in the galley, leaving everything spotless.

AKNOWLEDGEMENTS

Hurtigruten, Compagnie du Ponant, Jaime Borquez, Carlos Stroppa, Ilya Michael Hirsch, Miguel Olio, João Cordeiro, and Israel Klabin. The Lourenço Castanho School, Cecilia Perez, Jeannette de Vivo, Silvia Tuono, and Regina Abreu, who "forced" us to turn our vacation voyage into an environmental studies classroom.

M. Cassab, the first company that hired us to give a talk. Renata Borges and Maristela Colucci, who presented us with this literary challenge, and to all those who, directly or indirectly, helped us make this book a reality.

We especially want to thank our parents. Dad, it was you who led us to our own discovery of Antarctica and brought us safely home again. Mom, it is you who has always encouraged us to observe and fall in love with animals that live outside our windows. And we can't forget to thank our grandparents, who miss us horribly whenever we travel.

Tamara, Laura, Marina, and Marininha.

photo: Jaime Borquez

It was a lot of fun taking part in putting this book of memories together. We had to help the girls remember their stories and all the feelings that went with them. Writing was like sewing together all the scraps of memories and stories they had told us with so much excitement. Yet we had to ensure that the language was true to their personalities, joyful, scientific, and youthful. Working on this book was almost as challenging as a trip to Antarctica might be.

Selma Maria and João Vilhena

The most annoying part of the whole process of writing the book was that, to get to the meetings at the publisher's office, where we met with Selma, João, Renata, and Maristela, we first had to deal with the city of São Paulo's own version of the "Drake Passage" - traffic! We were usually almost asleep in the car by the time we arrived at the office. But then, as we told the stories of our memories, and as we wrote them out, we became so excited that we could hardly wait for the next meeting. It was thrilling to read the book as it was being created from the stories we told!

Laura, Tamara and Marininha Klink

ABOUT THIS BOOK

The first time we had the opportunity to take the girls "beyond the Convergence," Marininha was six years old and the twins were nine. That journey was life-changing for all of us.

By providing our children with this type of close-up contact with nature, in its original form, we noticed that they enjoyed discovering this world that is so different from the world in which we all live. Nature awakens in children new interests as they observe animals as they cross our paths. It is important for young people to learn to respect all forms of life and to understand the challenges of survival in a hostile climate.

The invitation by Grão Editora (our publisher) to produce this book was a wonderful surprise. It was written a bit differently and involved making sense of all the information the girls had collected on their trips. This arduous task befell Selma Maria, teacher of poetry and art, and Professor João Vilhena. They spent a lot of time talking with the girls, combing through their diaries, and looking at their drawings, and going through boxes and drawers full of scraps, photos and notes.

These professionals identified the highlights and best memories from five voyages to Antarctica. Together, we were able to organize the information into the chapters of this book.

My contribution to the project was in doing research over several years to determine what our daughters should know and learn when the time came to sail to one of the most incredible regions of our planet.

And here it is, in their voices. It is a summary of what they have learned. This book is unique, and is dedicated to both children and adults. We hope many people will learn from our daughters and become excited by their own discoveries.

We know that the future of the natural world is in the hands of today's children, who will soon be adults and able to help make this world an even better place to live.

Marina Bandeira Klink

ACKNOWLEDGMENTS

Instituto Baleia Jubarte (Humpback whale)
The mission of the Humpback Whale Institute is to preserve humpback whales and other cetaceous mammals in Brazil, seeking to harmonize human activities with the preservation of the our natural heritage.
www.baleiajubarte.org

Projeto Baleia Franca (Right whale)
The Right Whale Project is dedicated to research and conservation of right whales, the second most-threatened whale species. The Project's objective is to ensure the survival and recovery of the right whale population in Brazilian waters.
www.baleiafranca.org.br

Projeto Albatroz
The Albatross Project is a nongovernmental organization that was created because of the need to reduce the incidence of unintentional capture of marine fowl by maritime fishing activities. The Project conducts research aboard fishing vessels on the high seas, as well as environmental education for fishermen, encouraging the adoption of conservation measures in fishing routines. This is the only NGO in the world created exclusively to protect albatrosses and petrels at the risk of extinction.
www.projetoalbatroz.org.br

Projeto Tamar
The Tamar/ICMBio Project has been active in Brazil for over 30 years. Its mission is to promote the recovery of marine turtles and to conduct conservation actions, research, and social inclusion.
www.projetotamar.org.br

Aquário de Ubatuba (Aquarium)
The Ubatuba Aquarium was opened in 1996 by a group of oceanographers seeking to centralize research on conservation of the seas, as well as to inform and educate the public, recognizing the tremendous genetic and environmental potential contained in Brazil's rivers and coastal waters.
www.aquariodeubatuba.com.br

Aquário de Santos
The Santos Aquarium was the first Brazilian institution dedicated to the rescue and recovery of marine wildlife. The aquarium conducts significant work in environmental education, involving six million students per year. The aquarium is the second most visited park in the state of São Paulo and the oldest in Brazil (it opened in 1945). The aquarium is home to 2,000 species, from small invertebrates to sea mammals. Its attractions include sharks, groupers, *pacus*, rays, penguis and sea lions.
www.santos.sp.gov.br

Instituto Argonauta
The Argonaut Institute is a nongovernmental organization dedicated to marine conservation headquartered on the northern coast of the state of São Paulo, in the city of Ubatuba. The institute has worked in partnership with the Ubatuba Aquarium since 1998, conducting rescue and salvage of injured sea animals. The Center for Rehabilitation and Triage of Sea Animals (*Centro de Reabilitação e Triagem de Animais Aquáticos* – CRETA) was opened in 2005. This center treats penguins, dolphins, sea lions and other marine wildlife. In 2008 the center took in, recovered and returned to the sea about 600 Magellan penguins.
www.institutoargonauta.org